FACELESS MAN

A GOTHIC HORROR

ANAGHA GOPAN O G

Copyright © Anagha Gopan O G
All Rights Reserved.

I dedicate this story to all the Gods and Godessess.

I bow before Lord MahaVishnu and Devi MahaLakshmi.

Contents

Prologue

This is a fictional story. All the characters mentioned are hypothetical and fictionally constructed by the author. Similarity with any place or person in real life can only be considered as a coincidence.

PREFACE

"THE BOOK NARRATES HOW THE SPUN UP STORIES
TURNS INTO REALITY AFTER AN EXPEDITION BY
FATHER GREGON, JUDE AND FREON INTO HAUNTED
CASTLE"
-AUTHOR : Anagha Gopan O G

Acknowledgements

I feel grateful to release my story book. I thank Lord
Almighty for His blessings.
I, in advance, thank all the readers in and around the
globe for reading this story.

I
HAUNTED CASTLE

It all happened in Paris in 1780s in and around St. Peter's Catholic Church, situated in the hill top. The area attracts tourists due to its greenery as well as the miraculous happenings at the castle.

At the same time there is a highly restricted area for people in and around the castle except for the tribals named **Gotha**. Tourists often have access to these tribal huts where they are arranged food and protection from the wild creatures during the night time. The Gotha tribal head, whose name is Jude, is a seventy five year old man living with his family. He is a man of insights and faithful catholic who was a holy person, who preaches word of God to his tribal community.

Very often he gets inner voices pertaining to the devilish presence in the castle and he along with Father from St. Peter's Catholic Church and few tribals goes for prayers and necessary religious procedures so as to exhaust the devil's acts. There has been many instances of devil's presence abstraining the sacred procedures inside church.

Castle is quite a big one with several levels, including a basement and hidden underground hall. It is seemingly abandoned with no humans around its ten kilometers diameter circular yard. Around the castle is an orchard of apples. It is miraculous that in all the seasons the apples are produced. Apples both green and red, mostly green is seen throughout the year.

In the hall is the prayer room, where there is believed to be the presence of Greek Goddess, who takes rebirths to diminish the witches and devils haunting the castle .

Also beneath the bronze statue of the Greek Goddess there is a wooden door-like opening that leads to a dark tunnel. There begins the mouth of the secret tunnel, extending more than ten kilometres through the yard. The tunnel has its own flavour of haunt with it's branchings, claustrophobia and mystery.

As per Jude's words, it is very often that news channels cover information regarding the tunnel. The tunnel was once the secret passage for movement of goods. The tunnel was built by the Greeks who invaded the Catholic church area after a war and the castle was their store house of all the invaded items like jewelry, coins, antiques, gold, diamond mines and so on. At those times, Greek people used to loot the ornaments and disappear. The disappearance is into the tunnel which is on the halfway opening through a hole burrowed underneath, through trunk of a huge banyan tree. The hangings of the banyan tree along with rocks and shrubs keeps the entry into the tunnel out of sight. And of course, its more than a decade old.

The inner rooms in the castle have broken glass windows, spider webbed ceilings, rusted iron pillars, half turn stairs with the disconnected landing. Altogether it gives a picture of a haunted house with breeding reptiles like rats, rodents, cats, vowels, dogs etc.

A single room underneath the castle is full of coffins and dead bodies. And the key to the room is along with a bunch of five keys – three big keys which opens the lock of the room, hall and also entrance door of the castle. Other two keys which are smaller compared to the bigger one. Those smaller ones are which unlocks two secret doors at the beginning and the end of the tunnel.

****

II

FACELESS MAN

It was during the rein of Bishop Alphonse that people, even the other Fathers of the church followed strict and stringent rules.

Earlier the keys were secretly placed in a wardrobe inside the St. Peter's Catholic Church hall. No one except the Father who was appointed by the Bishop to take care of the keys had access to it. But Bishop had access to it. Even no one dared to question him. And also no one had excess to it. After the death of the Bishop, Father who was in charge of the keys left the holy church and castle keys to public opinion.

The villagers decided to keep the keys' with Jude only. He was well respected man in the community. He took the responsibility of the keys.

There were previously many suspicious as well as auspicious stories spun around the castle. Not all believed. Many felt as if being deceived to make them believe the stories and transform to historical incidents.

The entire story bought in different changes in minds of people and what they believe from then on.

It was after two months later Father Gregon took charge.

It was Father Gregon who changed the rules related to withholding the keys. Public went against him. He was unable to get any sort of support from common men, even Jude and the Gotha tribe.

He spoke to Jude regarding the keys and asked him for the keys. But Jude wasn't ready to hand over it to him. One day Father decided to go and visit the castle. From the public he came to know that the keys are with Jude. So he went to meet Jude.

"The keys are safe with me", said Jude.

"Is there any problem in handing over the key to me?", asked Father Gregon.

"Yes, of course. Definitely I cannot", replied Jude.

"I just want to visit the castle. Simply an expedition", said Father Gregon.

Father was provoking Jude very much. But just ended up in wasting time in getting the keys to keep with him. After so much of discussions, both came up with an idea of just going on an adventure to solve the mystery behind the castle. And of course regarding the rumors about the Faceless man.

The next day morning, Jude, his son Freon and Father Gregon left for the expedition. Jude carried a bible and a small holy cross with him. Even though he believed in God, he was frightened of what will happen next because that frightening was the spun up stories in reality.

Freon carried a torch light with him for he was sure of turning dark while returning back. And the castle as not lighted as per their knowledge. It was Father's and Freon's first visit to the castle. Unlike Jude who had previously been there with father Alphonse.

"Has anyone got any previous experience about visiting the castle?", Father Gregon asked.

"Yes, I have", said Jude.

"It is approximately 12 kilometers to walk into the castle", On the way Jude started describing his previous expedition with the Bishop to the castle and through the tunnel.

It was beyond a horror film plot. Something hidden is to be found out! But why it ended up in disaster? Its always a question that formed in common people's mind.

"Why did the Bishop suicide?", asked Father Gregon. "Wasn't it a mystery that the Father Khenion went on missing. Or did fate take the form of death in front of him? Anyway it sounds suspicious", he added.

Jude didn't reply directly to his questions. All were silent for two – three minutes.

****

III

SILVER KEYS

Jude reluctantly started the conversation by explaining his experiences on his visit.

"It was during a heavy rainy season, that I, along with Bishop, father Khenion and his choir boy Jeon left from my home early in the morning at 6 a m. Father Khenion was in charge of keeping the keys. It was my first visit to castle. I remember walking with a big umbrella which I holded for the Bishop as well as me. It was heavily raining along with thunder. We reached the small gateway which lead to an orchard. The gate was composed of half broken steel and iron pieces which was clinging on to rusted pillars on either sides. It's rust started powdering once we opened the gate. It was an orchard completely covered with trees and shrubs. Those tall grasses and weeds grown up made our journey a bit difficult. We had to make our way through such horrific and jungly orchard. On the way I remember we ourselves plucking out small shrubs and weeds with our hands. We did not carry any tools with us. Since it was our first visit, we barely had any prior-knowledge of anything. We moved forward towards the castle. Of course it was a destructed building. Pillars were damaged and it would at first sight give a ghostly circumstance. Almost home to crawling reptiles like mice, snails etc. We could also see bats flying over. It was more weird, than from stories heard from our forefathers, about the castle. We found it difficult to open the main door of the castle. After all we didn't know which exactly the key was. We had a bunch of five keys with us. And to be frank a single biggest of all keys left us a question, of which lock pairs it and what is unlocked by it?"

For sometime Jude went on for a pause in the conversation.

"Why were you so eager to keep the keys with you? And of course, I am suspecting you." Said Father Gregon putting his hands over the shoulders of Jude.

Jude just for a while trembled and was shocked.

"It was the opinion by the public and the church committee and I had to abide by their decision", said Jude.

He always kept keys in the pocket of his dress that he wears. He also made duplicate keys of the key set. And the original was replaced with the duplicate keys inside the wardrobe. The original were real Silver keys. None of them in public was aware of it.

By that time they had reached half the way to the castle. They stopped at a small tea shop. They ordered for tea for them to drink. Also there, they met few villagers who came near them and spoke to them.

"Tomorrow is a Friday. Few of us has decided to leave to the castle to see the faceless man. Even though we don't have access inside, we have decided to remain outside in the orchard and do our prayers. What if we happened to see the faceless man by then?", said a villager.

"The faceless man? It seems quite interesting. I would like to know more", said Father Gregon.

"Its all the spun up stories. We are trying to seek the truth. Father Khenion, once during a holy mass happened to explain about a man and his holy powers. He still exists it seems. Even father doubted whether he was the rebirth of Christ. He comes in various dressings. At times like a clown or wearing a suit or gown-like dress. It was quite amazing to hear those stuffs about him. But I think none of the villagers have had a chance to meet him. We donot know whether he is of any danger to common men", explained the owner of the tea shop. He was at the same time busy preparing tea for them.

"Is it like the man doesn't have a face?", asked father Gregon.

"The faceless man is just a name according to the description by people who has seen him. He covers his head with a clothing as if his head inside a wrapper. He wears a scarf, ribboned around the neck. Just like a spherical piece of chocolate wrapped in its covering. His face was not clearly visible to those who saw him, it seems", said Freon.

"Many spun up stories regarding the castle spread as like grandma tales. The most wide spread one being about the faceless man and the failed tries to find the truth behind the mysterious faceless man", said another villager.

Meanwhile, the tea shop owner gave the tea to them.

"The failed tries! That seems it would be such an adventurous story", said Father Gregon. And he continued, "we are on an expedition to the castle." He sips tea.

"Only during the Good Friday the entire atmosphere finds an upturn with human engagements. A day when people perform Prayers and celebrate the day with the unknown faceless man. Its all a day full of unexpected but wonderful changes in all those who gather, just like a miracle by the faceless man", explained Jude.

"Celebrations inside the castle! Who opens it for the public?", asked Father Gregon.

Father at the same time takes money from his pocket and pays to the tea shop owner.

Jude drank the tea and exclaims, "Only me!"

"There is another story. Its not a usual scene, people aren't frightened by him rather attract him to them. Just as if he is a friend. The very moment people sight him they faint. To their fortune, definitely not all, but those fearless awake to see him like a smiling clown's black face", explained Freon.

"Shall we move on? Have you all completed drinking the tea?", asked father.

"Yes, we will move. Let's not waste time through discussions." Said Freon.

They started walking towards the castle.

****

IV
INSIDE THE CASTLE

"Each and every incident count on to different experiences by different people. Most of the people who are adventure seekers, who go on for a challenge to seek the truth, often end up in dyeing inside the castle." explained Jude.

They reached near the broken gate of the castle. Freon opened the gate and they all moved forward. The orchard was fruitful. The shrubs and weeds made it difficult for them to pass through. The somehow found a way into the castle.

They reached the entrance door. Jude took the bunch of keys and tried keys one by one. At last one key opened the main door.

They entered inside the castle.

"Inside it has got many household items, though spider webbed and rusted." Said Freon.

Father took a wooden stick and started brooming off the webs. Freon was taking the households items one by one and looking on it.

"Those are the items which were looted once by the Greeks during their rein. There is a room in which is full of ornaments and jewelry. The district police force has taken measures to protect it from being looted from here", said Jude.

"So I guess those spun up stories has been made purposefully so as to deceive people and prevent them from visiting and looting the valuables from here", said Freon.

Father laughs.

In the very fraction of a minute something suspicious happened. It was nothing else but Freon lost his left arm. Father, Jude and Freon remained silent for a minute.

"Don't expect that we can go back alive", said Father Gregon.

Jude and Freon nodded their heads.

"Come what may. If at all fate takes my life, let it. Praise the Lord", cried Freon.

The very next moment he got his hand back. That was miraculous.

"Praise you Jesus", again cried Freon. He was unable to believe what has happened. But just praying and thanking Jesus for giving back his arms.

It was actually out of fear that they began praying together. Just a coincidence that they all started together.

"Our Father in heaven, Holy be Thy name, Your kingdom come, Your will be done on earth as in heaven. Give us today our daily bread...."

They were praying.

The moment they said the word *bread*, a bread loaf appeared in Freon's hand. Being so fast, unpredictable and feary, Freon threw it away from his hand. He did not even wait to see what it was. It all happened suddenly in seconds.

That was of course more frightening and they were speechless for minutes. After they experienced a voice of laughter. They tried to connect to the region from where it originated. They entered into the hall and found the statue of a Greek Goddess. It was made of bronze. They walked towards the statue. It was almost two metre in height. In front of the statue was a small plate which had a small lamp, some agarbhathi sticks, wicks and matchbox. Only that particular space had a sort of energy which can be felt unlike the other destructed regions of the castle. The scene showed a similarity to a old hindu mythology. He felt it almost like a clean Sancto sanctorium similar to those in temples.

Father Gregon tried to light the lamp. The match stick was not catching fire. Again and again he kept on trying to produce fire. But he failed. He felt awkward.

Just for once, he thought, was it because of being from a different religious community that was the block for lighting the lamp. May be the Goddess didn't like it. He was firm mythological believer and of course superstitious. Hence he felt it as a bad omen.

Just then a black cat jumped into the hall through somewhere and it's meow was again frightening for them. Altogether, the scenes watered their eyes, leaving them in a panic condition.

He left the matchbox back into the plate. While keeping it back he somehow slipped. For protection he just caught hold of the statue, which was involuntary action. To their surprise the bronze statue moved along with the wooden stand since it was on rolling wheels. It was clear that the statue covered the opening on the floor. On the floor there was a cupboard-like opening. It had a keyhole. Father fell again slipped on to the floor.

Jude and Freon helped Father to get up.

Outside it was raining heavily. There was strong wind with thunder and lightning. Their voice was not audible to each other at the normal volume they spoke. They had to raise their volume while speaking.

"Are you okay?", asked Freon to father.

"Yes, I am!", replied father Gregon.

They all took rest for sometime.

They just sat peacefully on the floor.

****

V

KENNY RHYION

Meanwhile Jude began narrating the heard story behind the suspicious death of Bishop Alphonse.

The story goes on spun in the convent of Bishop which left deserted after his death. Once, there was a time when it was shunned by the villagers and was devoutly visited by those travellers whom chance or curiosity came that way.

It was a day, the baptism day of Kenny Rhyion. The function went on smoothly. Prayer sections were well arranged and choir was led by Father Khenion. At the middle of the section, while the Bishop was directly carried out by him, a smoky cloud started forming. The atmosphere turned vulnerable. Outside the church dark clouds were seen to be filling up. Clouds bursted out, thunder and lightning accompanied. Rain showered. People from the streets and road, in order to escape the showering rain and thunder, ran to the church. The church was filled almost full. The sitout was becoming almost full. Electricity was cut off.

Noise could be heard from transformer cracking and bursting, aside the street.

Suddenly Father came out. He, along with other people outside the church noticed a figure forming over the clouds. They prepared themselves to experience something new. Many couldn't hold on to the breath. The scene was that much beautiful. As if someone mixing the colours to bring a new form out of it. Say, as like an abstract art.

Suddenly it turned out to be a human – like figure. Just as it appeared the entire day time elapsed to turn into a sudden, dark moonlight at night.

"Did the earth spin so fast, just for the sake of goodness?", Father Khenion was murmuring.

"Hope that today is not the end of the world", said a common man.

"A miraculous escape. Only God knows what is it?", said another.

People were discussing with each other. As the discussion went, someone was enquiring, what the hell was happening inside the church today? He was a disgusted man.

"Has it got something related to the child's birth? His name is Khenny Rhyion." Murmured a man.

"Spare him, for atleast thinking the he is a baby. I guess there's something which is turning the earth, like spinning a globe. Anyway, let us do some prayers together for the wellness of all. Atleast thank God, no harm for humans!", said another common man.

It was a suspicious moment in the lifetime. Father Khenion walked straight away to the Bishop. Together they discussed and began the prayer sections. That was a specially dedicated prayer section, to the Mother Mary.

They started and others joined, "*Hail Mary full of grace, the Lord is with you……*"

All ended up in automatically pointing up. Yes, it was like in statue of Liberty. That's what happened once they said the word 'you'.

Many turned wonder stuck in between prayers. They were unable to move. Turning still and motionless. They could feel the vibrating effect.

"Is this vibration due to prayers?", Father Khenion could only ask in public. There were many shivering.

But Bishop noted one thing. Only Khenny Rhyion was as usual happy. Rest all babies were effectively put on to suffer with others. From then on questions arose in his mind. Was actually Khenny's, a Godly birth? Or anything suspicious about him, anyway it's for his goodness??

They had to wind up the function.

"Everyone get ready for anything unexpected. Anything can happen at anytime. Time is running as usual. I thought it has stopped. Rather only forwarding of the earth's rotation. It was horrible. Such a horrible situation we had to face." Father Khenion announced through the mike to the people around.

Ready to face, coming what may, the crowd dispersed once the rain stopped and atmosphere calmed.

****

VI

FACELESS MAN

Just after a week was Christmas. Entire population was busy decorating their homes. Children were busy making up the Christmas tree and waiting for santa. A box full of sweets and chocolates were always worth waiting for and by the children.

But unfortunately everything changed and revolved around a twisty Christmas night which took the life of a fakely reputed unholy. He was Father Khenion in St. Peter's Catholic Church.

Serving more than 3 years as a Father, he lead a holy life. But the built up envies and jealous in and by the nuns in St. Peter's Convent winds him up into his death. Just their belief that he is dead rather than missing. The fake whispers and rumors about him took it outside the convent. People around started building up false notions about him. The very best quality of father is that he ignores all the unnecessary loose talks, even though he hears it.

Until the day when had to consider it seriously but it was too late. He was unable to.

"Was death too early? Or did the guardian angel protect him by giving him a new rebirth as a God?", said Bishop. His eyes watered while standing beside the coffin of Khenny. Unexpected departure left many questions again in front of Bishop and Father. Bishop felt it equivalent to a worse omen.

It was the third day from then on that Bishop suicided. He was totally stuck and unable to move and loss his bodily flexibility. He asked Father Khenion to give him poison. He left behind a small message stating not to take any such innocent lives since it's not less than a murder, just as a prayer note to Greek Goddess and suspiciously not to Jesus.

It was Rhyion and his wife who gave poison to Khenny. They found him loosing his hands and legs automatically. Khenny had totally turned lame and deaf also. Each day after the function was bad for him. They said they had a Godly vision and a faceless man appeared from somewhere and took away Kenny's soul with him. They couldn't do anything about it. Helpless, they prayed to God. It seems Khenny was rebirth of an evil in the form of a human. It seems that faceless man came to end him up. They, in fact trusted in faceless man.

****

VII

UNDERGROUND ROOMS

"What about Father Khenion?", asked Father Gregon.

"Let us keep the matter apart", smiled and said Freon.

All were sitting on the floor. Just then Freon got up.

Beneath the statue was a small wardrobe like structure built.

"Shall we open that wardrobe-like structure?", asked Freon. He tried opening it. But was unable to.

Jude then Jude got up and walked towards. He just examined the structure. He then took out the bunch of keys. One by one, he tried the keys to the lock hole. But was unable to.

"None of the keys opens this lock", he said.

"We will search for it's key inside the castle. What if it's kept hidden somewhere inside here?", explained father Gregon and he stood up.

Within minutes they took their own way into different direction to search for the key.

Father walked straight to a room. Jude followed him. The key of the room was with Jude. They opened the room and there was an almirah. Jude opened the almirah and took a large silver key.

He went near the lock and opened the opening to the basement. They three climbed down to the basement and found a chamber. The chamber had a small opening which was locked. They neglected it.

Jude took the bunch of keys from his pocket and opened the door to the room. Alas! It was empty.

"It's safer if we had few people, especially magicians, with us. I mean black magicians. Let's go back now and return some other day. Any witch-like activities inside the castle has to be dealt seriously.", said Father.

Leaving the expedition half-way, they decided to leave back to their house. They placed large silver key back in the almirah and closed it.

They made sure nothing was misplaced from the castle. They walked back. Meanwhile, Father, before Jude locking the main door, rushes into the castle back to get that silver key. He took it from there and kept in his pocket. Others didn't know why he went inside, nor did they ask.

After father came out, Jude locked the door and they all dispersed.

****

VIII

SAPERE AUDE

It was a New Year night when father Gregon gets an anonymous insight which was nearing his death. It was like a warning to him that he will be murdered. He woke up suddenly from the bad dream. He keeps the matter apart and zips the last portion of the wine and goes flat on the bed, into a very deep sleep.

It was after half an hour that the calling bell rang. It was Jude who was waiting outside to meet father. He was there to inform him about the group of students coming to invade the castle.

Father got up and Jude explained everything in detail. The day went off.

On the next day morning, Joel , a choir boy who sings for church prayers finds the Father missing from his room. He searched for him in church, orchard and nearby places as much as he could. Finally Father was confirmed as missing.

The church was left doubtfully empty. Devotees left the church unable to attend the holy mass. The missing news of the Father soon spread like a forest fire. Search for him began by local people and police ended up in vain.

People hated Father Gregon for he just ignored the opinions of the common and was strict in his own way. But the situation turned worst when Joel's body was found hanging upside down, outside the castle on a tree. He had left to castle in search of Father. But he could'nt return lively. It left many unsolvable questions among public. Near by his body was a note carved on a rock. ***"Sapere aude"***. *It was a Latin word.* It left the castle and the orchard being abandoned even by Jude. Father Gregon and Jude, decided to go find the truth. They decided to get the help of few magical students, as if, it might help them.

****

IX

CAGED CROW

Brennon was a handsome, hedonistic lad of early twenties. He had been learning magic right from age of twelve from *Magical Tricky University* at Paris. Upon turning into twenty years of age, the built up envies within his filthy classmates pretending to be friends faked him as a witch. But he wasn't. Rather he was an innocent magician whose smartness left the accompanied ones unanswerable in front of him. He was very often mistrusted even by parents.

At times he felt all the tricks and the magical winds and books left untouchable. Whatever he learnt were expected to be caged. Everything being remaining as a mere dream.

At his home, he had two pets tiger and a crow. Both were caged. The fierce tiger was only friendly with him and his family. While the crow was always in a small cage. It was the very unusual pets among humans. They were his only friends in due course of time.

Too much of loneliness left him face weird life. It was intolerable for men like him. He was highly under depression and often exploded in his words with whomever he aboarded, though rarely. He was very weak in controlling his emotions both psychologically and mentally. He also doubted if he looses memory very often. Mere non-sense.

"Go on for a filmy plot with your life as a story", his father used to comment.

"If it's like forgetting to switch off the electric appliances after it's usage, as it's common disorder for all", said his mother.

Brennon was adamant regarding his doubts and decided to go consult a doctor. Parents were not completely supporting.

"Don't let your innocense destroy your life", said his father. He was striken by his words. He took back the decision to consult doctor.

One day he was searching for his magical ring. It was not in the place where it was kept. Searching for too long time, atlast he got in the memory, the scene after feeding the crow. Yes, it was in the cage. He found it clung on to the feet of the crow. Brennon was a handsome, hedonistic lad of early twenties. He has been learning magic right from age of twelve. Upon turning into twenty, the built up envies within his filthy classmates pretending to be friends faked him as a witch. He was very often mistrusted even by parents. At times he felt all the tricks and the magical winds and books left untouchable. Whatever he learnt were expected to be caged.

He had two pets tiger and a crow. Both were caged. The fierce tiger was only friendly with him and his family. While the crow was always in a small cage, the very unusual pet among humans. He was highly under depression and often exploded in his words with whomever he aboarded, though rarely. He was very weak in controlling his emotions both psychologically and mentally. He also doubted if he looses memory very often. Mere non-sense.

"Go on for a filmy plot with your life as a story", his father used to comment.

"If it's like forgetting to switch off the electric appliances after it's usage, it's a common disorder for all", said his mother.

Brennon was adamant regarding his doubts and decided to go consult a doctor. Parents were not completely supporting.

"Don't let your innocence destroy your life. And remember, it will be more and enough for the filthy friends around you to discuss and laugh at", said his father. He was striken by his words. He took back the decision to consult doctor.

One day he was searching for his magical ring. It was not in the place where it was kept. Searching for too long time, atlast he got in the memory, the scene after feeding the crow. Yes, it was in the cage. He found it clung on to the feet of the crow. He just took the ring and wore it.

****

X

TRIP FROM COLLEGE

It was the New Year eve. He along with three others, were selected based on the marks obtained, for an expedition. It was for a casestudy to the castle at Paris.

On January 3rd they were to leave for the expedition from the University.

Alex, Jerin, and Brennon gathered in the campus. Juna was a little late. They had to write a report after their visit. After Juna reached, they along with one of their tutor as leader, left for seeking Jude.

One day they spend with Jude on reaching Jude's home. That was their first experience staying in a tribal community. Jude made arrangements for them to stay in their hut and also served them food.

While it became dusk, the tribals gathered for a meeting. The new expedition team and whether to allow them go to the castle was the major area of their discussion. The gang introduced them to the tribals and arranged themselves to show few magics as they were all the aspiring magical students. Also it was their first experience watching a tribal dance.

After the tribal dance, they had food. It was a special chicken fry along with chapatis. The dinner was fine along with the glass of grape wine. After that they all dispersed for sleeping.

Time passed by. It was early in morning 4 a m. Jude woke up. He refreshed himself and started his usual prayers. Brennon woke up by that time. He went to others and woke them up.

"Guys, get up!", he yelled so as to ensure all woke up. One by one, they refreshed themselves and got ready for the expedition.

By that time, Jude completed his prayers and reached back to them. He also was getting ready for leaving.

Finally at 5.30 a m, they all left from Jude's home.

They had already taken the breakfast and packed their lunch.

On the way Father Gregon joined them.

"Praise the Lord", they exclaimed to the Father. Father smiled and replied the same to them.

Happily they moved forward.

On the way Jude started narrating story of Father Khenion.

"This expedition is going to be more than an experience. It's risky. You are risking life. Its only a couple of days back, one of the choir boy hanged in front of the castle. Anyway, I doubt that the dead body is still there, untouched by others. The miraculous and strange stories are to be unmasked. It seems frightening. Last expedition was canceled midway by us. Let it not happen this time. I hope you magicians are not witches.", explained Father Gregon.

"No we, aren't witches. Rather students learning magic. That's all", replied Juna.

"The news in television channels seem rare nowadays. Penguins are loosing their own Wings. Unable to migrate for their own life. Polar bears unable to hibernate and are almost dying below the ozone hole layer in Antarctica. Drastic temperature variation into 23 degree Celsius were beyond tolerance for the native species. There has been massive species destruction as per NatGeo channel report. There has been satellite images and videos showing the Same. The white, snowy region turning into blood red. It so strange that species are attacking their own home native species. Killing others to make food for them. Massive self destruction going on. Thanks to God, that Antarctica is unoccupied by humans", explained Brennon.

"Just as day shifted to night. Sudden changes need not be adaptable for animals and birds. Or any other mammals. Unlike humans. Anyway the changes in the universe is inevitable. Come what may. Be it good or bad", explained Father Gregon.

"let's wait and see. Any way it's a matter far beyond our control.", explained Brennon.

They reached near by the gate. It was left open. They entered the orchard. On the way young, magician team tried plucking apples. It was a quite different moment, plucking those green apples. They just put the plucked apples in their bags. Meanwhile, Father Gregon and Jude was simply standing watching the team plucking apples.

Once they completed plucking the possible apples, they decided to move on.

"Yeah! Now we will move on.", said Jerin.

They were enthusiastic gang. They walked on and reached the castle. Jude opened the entrance door.

"Oh!! It seems so old. A bit frightening, seeing the interior Outlook.", said Alex.

"We will straight away move to the idol of the Greek Goddess. Let's see how to proceed". Said Father Gregon. Jude opened the door to underground room.

"One key opened a room which was full of dead bodies. The mummies. The mummified stories have been a hot topic of discussions. Reality was quite frightening than expected. I remember the very first day of venture into this castle.", exclamed Jude.

Meanwhile, Alex and Juna were trying to go upstairs.

"Hey, Alex and Juna keep your feet away. Don't stamp on the stairs. Its all rusted", said a voice.

"Who??, Who who was that? Didn't you hear someone speaking? Said Juna. "Yah! Our names were being called upon! But I think. It's him the faceless man. Its disgusting. I am........ I am not...Help!!! ".

In the very next moment everyone ran and gathered around Alex. There lies Alex fainted on the floor. Brennon took some water and sprinkled on Alex's face. He shook his body and face. But it was of no use.

"I just heard a voice speaking and also sound of him yelling before fall.", said Juna.

They all patiently waited for Alex to wake up.

"Shall I give a try? Otherwise he will not", said again a voice.

"Whoever it is please come in front of us. We are ready to face you"...said Father Gregon.

Suddenly there was smoke spreading around the statue of Greek Goddess... As if in a manner, colours mixing on a pellete with water, there appeared some strange scenes . There appeared a man. He wore a black dress. He had a ribbon like a tie in his neck. He had no legs. He was like a jinnie which came out of the statue.

He was flying as he wish through out inside the castle. Suddenly, he came and stopped near father Gregon.

"Alex is dead. Don't panic. And just a warning that don't be over smart to find the truth. Most of the stories about me are spun up. I can help you narrating anything you wanna know. Better you quit the expedition. Don't go too much into the underground channels.."

Again this time too, the gang decided to return back. They took the body of Alex and sobbed. Slowly they moved out of the castle.

Again that added to another story of leaving back the truths behind faceless man and haunted castle....

****

About The Author

Author is Anagha Gopan O G, a civil engineering graduate from Cochin University of Science and Technology. She is a passionate writer and a bibliophile.

Other publications by the author-

1. SOUL-HUMAN INTERACTION by Notion Press

2. MY SPIRITUAL WINGS by Notion Press

3. EUHORIA september 2021 Anthology under Quill house

Thanks for reading,

Anagha Gopan O G

****